50¢

Based on the TV series *SpongeBob SquarePants*® created by
Stephen Hillenburg as seen on Nickelodeon®

SIMON SPOTLIGHT
An imprint of Simon & Schuster Children's Publishing Division
1230 Avenue of the Americas, New York, New York 10020
Copyright © 2005 Viacom International Inc. All rights reserved.
NICKELODEON, *SpongeBob SquarePants,* and all related titles, logos,
and characters are registered trademarks of Viacom International Inc.
All rights reserved, including the right of reproduction in whole
or in part in any form.
SIMON SPOTLIGHT and colophon are registered trademarks of
Simon & Schuster, Inc.
Manufactured in Mexico
Abridged Edition
4 6 8 10 9 7 5
ISBN 978-1-4169-0291-1
0210 RR6

Go, Graduate!

All the Best from Bikini Bottom

by David Lewman

Simon Spotlight/Nickelodeon
New York London Toronto Sydney

You read all the right books!

You really kept it together!

Sure,
maybe you got behind once or twice,
BUT YOU DID IT!

Great job, pardner!
Graduatin' can be tougher than
wrestlin' a giant clam!

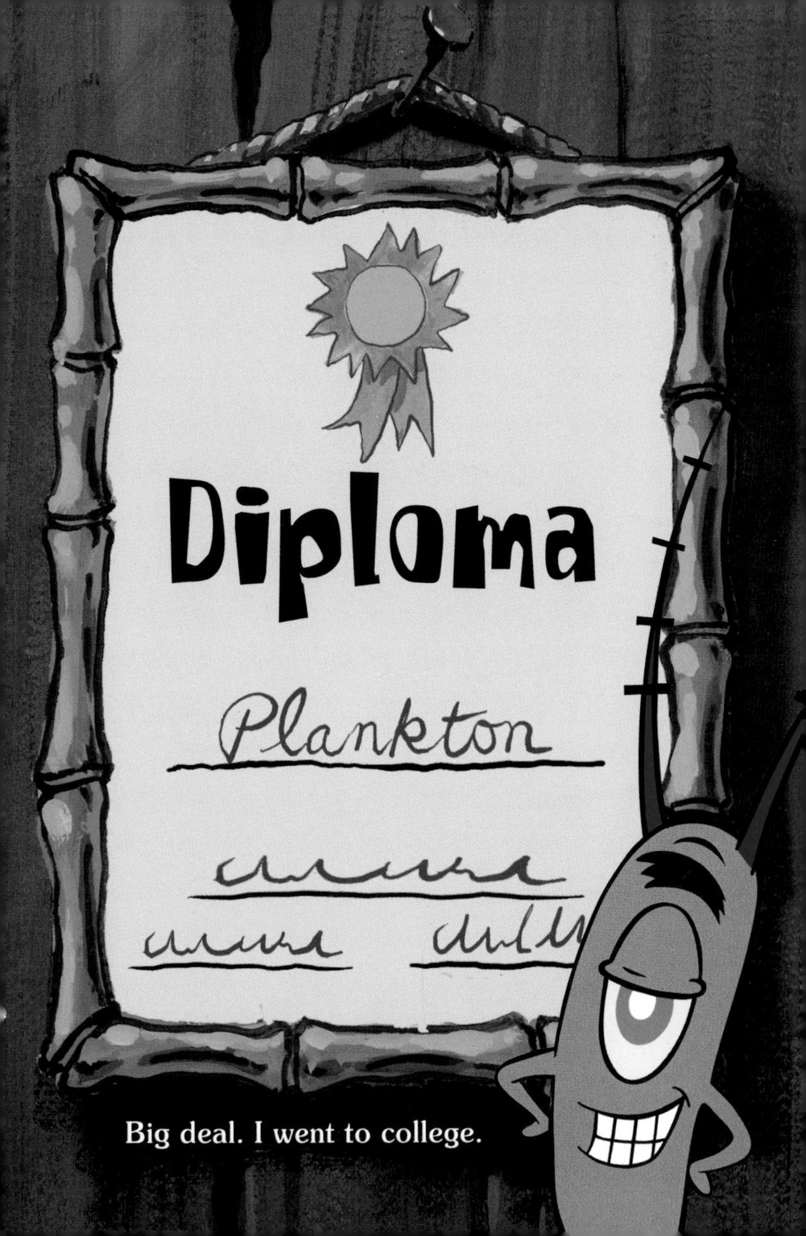
Diploma
Plankton
Big deal. I went to college.

TIPS FOR THE BIG DAY

First things first:
You'll want to be very clean for graduation.

You'll want to get dressed up.

And please go to the bathroom

before

the ceremony.

I haven't graduated from Mrs. Puff's boating school yet, but someday, when I do, I'll know just what to say in my graduation speech!

Fellow boating-school graduates, we've been through a lot together—a lot of boating. We've boated forward, and we've boated backward. We've boated to the right, and we've boated to the left, which I still have trouble with.

But thanks to the greatest boating teacher in the world, Mrs. Puff, we've learned how to boat with the best of boaters ... boatily.

So let me just say in conclusion that
I'M READY ... TO DRIVE A BOAT!

Come on, fellow boaters, let's get out there and boat!

Thank you.

THE BEST PART OF GRADUATING:
THE CELEBRATION!

You'll figure out the best way to celebrate your graduation, because you're a deep thinker.

You've worked hard, graduate.
How about a party? With live music, of course!

With so many possibilities and choices to make, you may feel like you are having a hard time standing on two feet.

But just remember that life after graduation is full of surprises—you never know what you might find!

Maybe someday you'll be . . .

a doctor . . .

or maybe a lawyer.

Maybe you'll own a business and make boatloads of money!

Or if you're really lucky,
you'll land the greatest
job of all—working at the
Krusty Krab!

GRADUATE, I SALUTE YOU.

Go have some fun. And remember,
no matter what you decide to do next . . .

you're sure to be a
star.